Hello Dancer!

EMAN
BOOKS

You shine like a star when you move to the beat.

Watching you dance is always a treat.

Dancing is fun, puts a smile on your face,

Twirling and leaping in your happy place.

Each day in class, your hard work makes you better.

Doing your best shows us you're a go getter.

You practise and practise while counting the moves,

Across the dance floor in your special dance shoes.

Ballet dancers plié (plee-ay), sauté (soh-tay), and jeté (zhuh-tay).

With graceful and strong moves

of muscular play.

The taps on your shoes make cool

sounds with your feet.

Like shuffle ball-change,

brush dig heel, then repeat.

Hip hop class wakes you up,

Puts you in a great mood.

To pop, lock, and slide,

Feed your body smart food.

Jazz hands, step ball change,

Jazz square, grapevine.

Your effort and hard work

Pay off so you shine.

You're a dancing machine and you sparkle with joy!

Your good vibes in class spread to each girl and boy.

Feel the beat and the rhythm,

Your heart dancing with it.

It's easy to tell that you love every minute.

The music is ready. Try not to be late.

Teacher counts your class in with 5,6,7,8.

Sometimes you hear, "It's not working, please stop.

Let's try it again and start from the top."

18

Helping each other remember the moves.

All dancing the same as everyone grooves.

Listening and learning to what teacher knows.

You make dancing magic with your twinkle toes.

At the end of the class, if there's time left for play,

Teacher says, "Free dance, the rest of today."

Keen dancers cheer loudly. The music begins.

You make up cool steps, groovy leaps, and fast spins.

The big day is coming and now is the chance,

To finish small details of your special dance.

Put on your costume, it's time to run through

The steps and routines you might need to review

To work out the problems and see how things go.

Weird things could happen, you just never know.

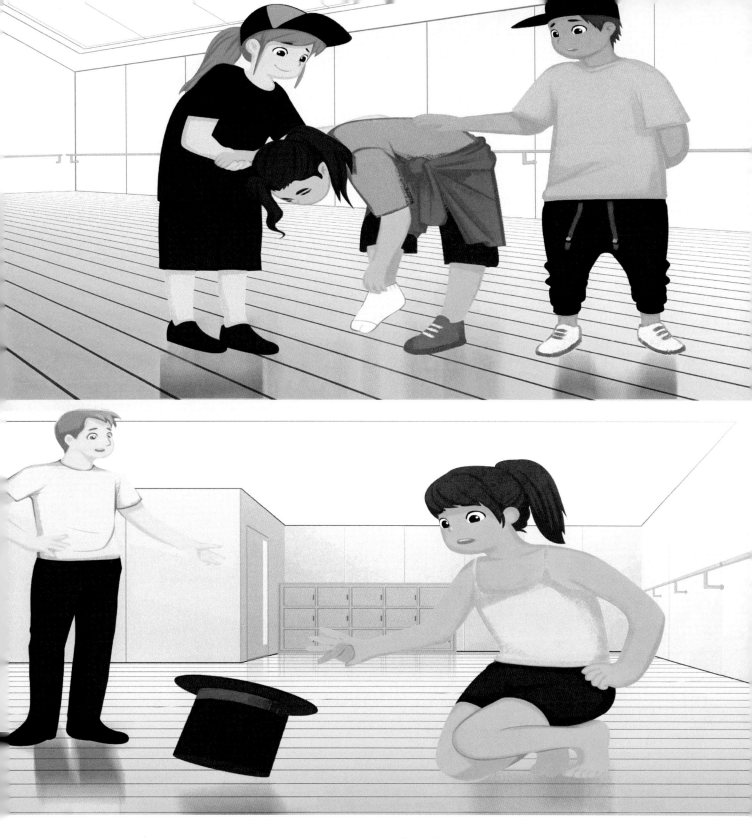

A trip-up or slip-up might happen to you.

Your team will help out. It's what good friends do!

A costume could break, or the music won't play.

Or the dance is forgotten, it all is okay! 23

As you take the stage on the very last day,

Looking great in your costume and dancing away.

It's okay to be nervous. It's normal to do.

Smile. Share your style. Have some fun and be you!

When the dance year is over,

it's time for a rest.

Be proud of your effort,

'Cause you did your best!

My Dancing Feet

What do I want to learn this year?

What should I remember to do every time I dance?

What are some things I am good at?

My Dancing Feet

What are some things I want to get better at?

What am I working on at practise?

What do I like best about dancing?

Dance Memories

Year:

Dance Team Name:

Dance Teacher's Name:

Dancers in my Group:

Where did I perform?

What was my favourite performance? Why?

What is my favourite dance? Why?

Dance Team Autographs

Dance Team Autographs

Autographs

Autographs

Draw a picture of yourself dancing!

Draw a picture of your dance teacher!

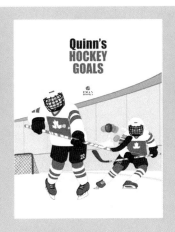

Manufactured by Amazon.ca
Bolton, ON

22470302R00024